Snow White

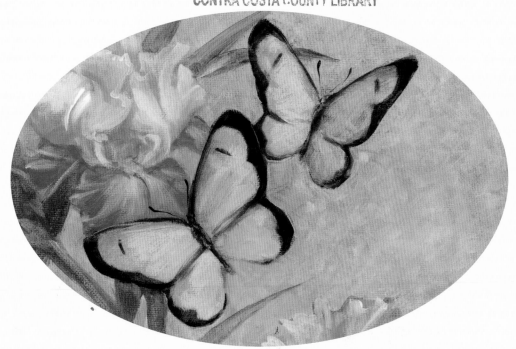

Melinda Cop

DUTTON CHILDREN'S BOOKS

For my mom, who let me keep a lot of the little dwarfs
that followed me home from the pet store
and then kept the drawings I made of them

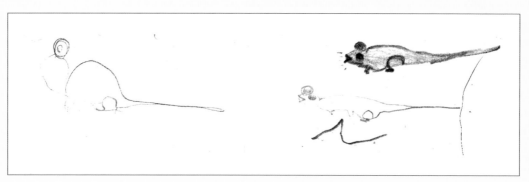

The artist's drawings of special mouse friend Cutie Pie (age 5)

Special thanks to Yvonne MacKinnon for her beautiful Celtic-inspired ceramic designs,
and to my husband, Bob, for all his magical technical help.

DUTTON CHILDREN'S BOOKS
A DIVISION OF PENGUIN YOUNG READERS GROUP
PUBLISHED BY THE PENGUIN GROUP • PENGUIN GROUP (USA) INC., 375 HUDSON STREET, NEW
YORK, NEW YORK 10014, U.S.A. • PENGUIN GROUP (CANADA), 10 ALCORN AVENUE, TORONTO,
ONTARIO, CANADA M4V 3B2 (A DIVISION OF PEARSON PENGUIN CANADA INC.) • PENGUIN
BOOKS LTD, 80 STRAND, LONDON WC2R 0RL, ENGLAND • PENGUIN IRELAND, 25 ST STEPHEN'S
GREEN, DUBLIN 2, IRELAND (A DIVISION OF PENGUIN BOOKS LTD) • PENGUIN GROUP
(AUSTRALIA), 250 CAMBERWELL ROAD, CAMBERWELL, VICTORIA 3124, AUSTRALIA (A DIVISION OF
PEARSON AUSTRALIA GROUP PTY LTD) • PENGUIN BOOKS INDIA PVT LTD, 11 COMMUNITY
CENTRE, PANCHSHEEL PARK, NEW DELHI - 110 017, INDIA • PENGUIN GROUP (NZ), CNR
AIRBORNE AND ROSEDALE ROADS, ALBANY, AUCKLAND 1310, NEW ZEALAND (A DIVISION OF
PEARSON NEW ZEALAND LTD) • PENGUIN BOOKS (SOUTH AFRICA) (PTY) LTD, 24 STURDEE
AVENUE, ROSEBANK, JOHANNESBURG 2196, SOUTH AFRICA • PENGUIN BOOKS LTD, REGISTERED
OFFICES: 80 STRAND, LONDON WC2R 0RL, ENGLAND

Published in the United States by Dutton Children's Books,
a division of Penguin Young Readers Group
345 Hudson Street, New York, New York 10014
www.penguin.com/youngreaders

Designed by Irene Vandervoort

Manufactured in China
First Edition
ISBN 0-525-47474-9
10 9 8 7 6 5 4 3 2 1

ONCE UPON A TIME, in the middle of winter, as snowflakes fell like feathers from the sky, a Queen sat gazing out her window. Through its black ebony frame she admired the blooming bush planted outside. The pink of its blossoms looked so beautiful against the white snow that the Queen thought, *If only I had a child as white as snow, as pink as a blossom, and as black as the wood of the window frame.*

Soon after, she gave birth to a little daughter with fur as white as snow, a nose as pink as a blossom, and ears as black as ebony. The child was called Snow White, and right after she was born, the Queen died.

A year went by, and the king took another wife. The new Queen was beautiful, but vain and haughty, and she could not tolerate any other who rivaled her beauty. She had a magic mirror and often stood in front of it, admired herself, and said:

> *Mirror, mirror, on the wall,*
> *who in this land is fairest of all?*

Then the mirror would answer:

> *You, my Queen, are fairest of all.*

And with this reply the Queen would be content, for she knew the mirror always told the truth.

Time passed, and Snow White grew up and became more and more beautiful. She became as lovely as the day is clear and more handsome than the Queen herself. So one day, when the Queen asked the mirror:

> *Mirror, mirror, on the wall,*
> *who in this land is fairest of all?*

And the mirror answered:

> *You, my Queen, have a beauty quite rare,*
> *but Snow White is many times more fair.*

The Queen was horrified. From that moment, envy and pride grew in her heart like weeds every time she laid eyes on young Snow White. Finally, she could stand it no longer.

The Queen summoned a huntsman and said, "Take Snow White away into the woods and kill her, for I can no longer bear the sight of her. When you return, bring me her heart so that I may have proof of the deed."

The huntsman dared not disobey, so he led Snow White deep into the woods. He drew his hunting knife to pierce her heart, but Snow White began to weep and pleaded with him to spare her life. The huntsman, touched by her beauty, took pity on Snow White and let her go. Just then, a wild boar rushed by, and the huntsman killed it, taking its heart for the Queen as proof.

Poor Snow White was now all alone in the wild wood. She was so frightened that she trembled at every leaf that rustled on the trees. So she began to run, and she ran on and on until finally she came to a little cottage and went inside to rest.

Everything in the cottage was tiny, neat, and clean. Upon a white-covered table were seven little plates. Beside the plates lay seven little forks, seven little knives, seven little spoons, and seven little tankards. Against the wall, side by side, stood seven little beds.

Snow White was so hungry and so thirsty that she took a bit of food from each of the seven plates and a sip from each of the seven tankards. When she had finished, she was so tired that she tried each little bed, one by one. No single tiny bed fit quite right, so she lay across three all at once. That suited her perfectly, and she soon fell fast asleep.

Night fell, and the owners of the little cottage returned. They were seven dwarfs who worked in the mountains, mining for gold. The dwarfs lit seven candles and discovered that someone had been in their home.

"Who has been sitting in my chair?" said the first dwarf.

"Who has been eating off my plate?" said the second.

"Who has been eating my bread?" said the third.

"Who has been eating my vegetables?" said the fourth.

"Who has been using my fork?" said the fifth.

"Who has been cutting with my knife?" said the sixth.

"Who has been drinking from my tankard?" said the seventh.

Then the first dwarf looked about the cottage and saw that his bed was rumpled. "Who has been sleeping in my bed?" he said. The others ran to their beds. Snow White was soon discovered, lying across three little beds, fast asleep.

When the dwarfs saw the girl, they cried out in surprise. Each fetched a little candle so that they might see her better. So pleased were they by her beauty that they let the girl sleep on through the night.

When the sun rose the next morning, Snow White awoke. How frightened she became when she saw the seven little dwarfs! But they were friendly and asked, "What's your name?"

"My name is Snow White," she answered.

"And what has brought you to our home?" they asked.

So Snow White told the dwarfs her story. She told them about her cruel stepmother, who had ordered Snow White to be killed, and about the huntsman who had spared her life and how her journey in the wild wood had brought her to their cottage. Then the dwarfs said to Snow White, "If you will care for our house, cook for us, make our beds, wash our clothes, and keep everything neat and clean, then you may stay with us, and you will want for nothing."

"Yes," Snow White agreed. "With all my heart."

And so Snow White stayed with them and kept their house. The dwarfs left early each morning to mine the mountains, and when they returned in the evening, their food was waiting for them. Snow White remained alone during the day, and the dwarfs warned her to be careful. "Beware of your stepmother. She will soon discover that you are here. Do not let anyone in."

The Queen, meanwhile, believing that Snow White was dead—and that she herself was now the most beautiful in the land—went again to her mirror and asked:

Mirror, mirror, on the wall,
who in this land is fairest of all?

And the mirror answered:

You, my Queen, have a beauty quite rare,
but Snow White is many times more fair.
Over the hills, and far away,
she dwells with the seven dwarfs today.

The evil Queen was furious, for she knew that the mirror always spoke the truth, and she realized at once that the huntsman had deceived her. Once again, her thoughts were consumed by plots to kill Snow White. The Queen would have no peace until she was again the most beautiful in the land. At last she came upon an idea. She painted her face and disguised herself as an old peddler woman so that she could not be recognized, then set out for the dwarfs' cottage.

"Good things for sale!" cried the Queen when she arrived outside the cottage.

Snow White peeped through the window. "Good day, my good woman. What have you to sell?" she asked.

"Pretty things, my dear. Silken laces of every color." She held one up.

I can let this honest old woman in, thought Snow White. *Surely the dwarfs would not mind.* And so she opened the door and bought a pretty lace.

"My dear, let me lace you up properly." Snow White allowed the Queen to fasten her bodice with the silken lace. But the Queen tied the lace so tightly that Snow White could not breathe, and she fell down as though dead.

"Now *I* am the most beautiful again!" declared the Queen, and she hurried away.

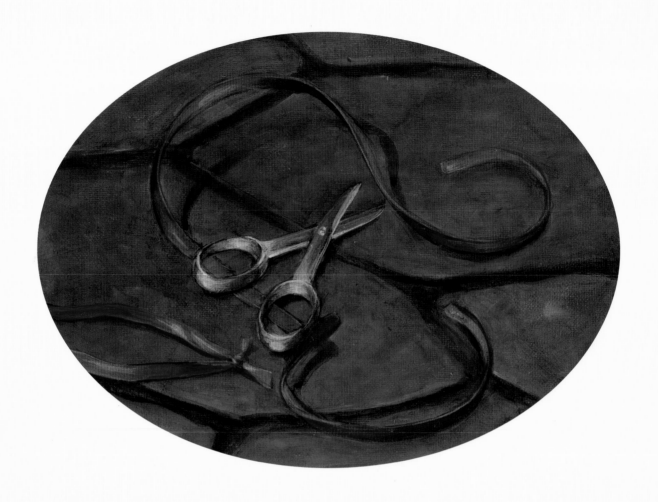

When evening came, the seven dwarfs came home and found Snow White lying upon the ground. They lifted her up and saw at once how tightly the lace was tied and cut it in two. Snow White drew a long breath and slowly came back to life.

When the dwarfs heard Snow White's tale, they understood at once what had happened. "That old woman was the evil Queen," they told Snow White. "Mind what we told you and let no one in while we are away."

As soon as the wicked Queen arrived home, she went to her mirror and asked:

> *Mirror, mirror, on the wall,*
> *who in this land is fairest of all?*

And the mirror answered:

> *You, my Queen, have a beauty quite rare,*
> *but Snow White is many times more fair.*
> *Over the hills, and far away,*
> *she dwells with the seven dwarfs today.*

When she heard this, the blood rushed to her head, and the Queen realized that Snow White must have been brought back to life.

"I will get her yet," she swore.

So the Queen made a poisonous comb and, once again disguising herself, made the journey to the dwarfs' cottage.

"Pretty things for sale!" she cried.

Snow White looked out the window. "I must not let anyone in," she said.

"Surely you are allowed to look," said the disguised Queen. She held up the comb—beautiful, but poisoned.

There can be no harm in just looking, thought Snow White when she saw the pretty comb. And so she opened the door and bought it.

"My dear, let me comb your fur properly." Snow White allowed the Queen to fix her fur with the poison comb. As soon as the comb had touched Snow White's ears, the poison began to work, and she fell down as if dead.

"Now you are done at last!" declared the wicked Queen. And she hurried away.

Luckily, the seven dwarfs soon came home and found Snow White lying upon the ground. They guessed that Snow White's evil stepmother had visited once again. They discovered the poison comb and drew it out, and Snow White immediately began to recover. One more time, they warned Snow White to open the door to no one.

As soon as the wicked Queen arrived home, she went to her mirror and asked:

> Mirror, mirror, on the wall,
> who in this land is fairest of all?

And the mirror answered:

> You, my Queen, have a beauty quite rare,
> but Snow White is many times more fair.
> Over the hills, and far away,
> she dwells with the seven dwarfs today.

Upon hearing this, the evil Queen shook with rage. "Snow White shall die!" she declared. "Even if it costs me my own life!" And she went into a secret chamber and created a poisonous apple. It was beautiful to behold, pearly white on one side and rosy red on the other. So powerful was the Queen's magic that anyone who looked at the apple would desire it, but would die after a single bite.

The Queen disguised herself one more time and set out for the dwarfs' cottage. She knocked on the door.

Snow White put her head out the window and said, "Old woman, I must not allow anyone in. The dwarfs have forbidden it."

"I do not need to come in," said the disguised Queen. "Here, let me give you one of these fine apples. It is a present."

"Oh, no!" said Snow White. "I must not take it."

"Are you afraid of poison?" asked the Queen. "See here, I will cut this apple in two. You may take the rosy red half, and I will eat the white half myself."

But the apple was so cleverly made that only the red half was poisoned. So tempting was the apple that when she saw the old woman eating it, Snow White thought there could be no danger, and she accepted the poisoned half. No sooner had she tasted it than she fell down dead.

The wicked Queen laughed a horrible, wretched laugh and cried, "White as snow, pink as a blossom, black as ebony. This time not even the dwarfs will be able to wake you!"

She hurried home and asked the mirror:

> *Mirror, mirror, on the wall,*
> *who in this land is fairest of all?*

And the mirror answered:

> *You, my Queen, are fairest of all.*

And her evil, envious heart found rest.

That night, when the dwarfs came home, they found Snow White lying dead on the ground. They lifted her tenderly and searched for the object that might have caused the harm. They unlaced her bodice, combed her hair, washed her with water and wine, but it was all in vain. Dear Snow White was dead, and dead she would remain.

The dwarfs laid her on a bier, and all seven wept at her side for three whole days. They wanted to bury her, but she looked so fresh and her nose remained so rosy — as if she were still alive. "We cannot hide her away in the dark earth," they said.

So the dwarfs built a coffin of glass and laid her in it so she could be seen on all sides. They chiseled Snow White's name in letters of gold and wrote that she had been the daughter of the king. The dwarfs carried the coffin up to the top of the mountainside and stood guard over it. The animals, too, came to weep for Snow White: first an owl, then a raven, and then a little dove.

Snow White lay in the coffin for a long, long time. Her body did not decay; she only looked to be sleeping and remained ever beautiful: white as snow, pink as a blossom, black as ebony.

It happened one day, much later, that a handsome prince discovered the coffin on the mountain, saw what was written in golden letters, and became entranced by Snow White.

"If you let me have the coffin," he said to the dwarfs, "I will give you anything you ask."

"We could not sell it for all the gold in the world," said the dwarfs.

"Then let me have it as a gift, for I cannot live without seeing Snow White," said the prince. "I will treasure her more dearly than any possession."

The good dwarfs pitied him and his words moved them, so they gave him the coffin. The prince's servants picked up the coffin and placed it upon their shoulders to carry it away, but they stumbled, and the jolt shook loose the bit of poison apple from Snow White's throat.

She opened her eyes and sat up, alive once again.

"Where am I?" asked Snow White.

"You are with me," replied the prince, who told her all that had happened. "I love you more than anything in the world. Come with me to my father's palace and be my queen."

And Snow White loved him, too, and went with him, and their wedding was arranged with much glory and splendor.

And what of Snow White's
evil stepmother? She was invited
to the wedding feast,
and as soon as she arrived,
the Queen recognized Snow White.
Her heart burst from rage,
and she dropped down dead.

The End